G000153721

DIV~~IDED~~
WE FALL

A SUSSEX CRIME SHORT STORY

By Isabella Muir

Published in Great Britain
By Outset Publishing Ltd

Published December 2018

Copyright © Isabella Muir 2018

Isabella Muir has asserted her right under the Copyright, Designs and
Patents Act 1988 to be identified as the author of this work.

All characters in this publication are fictitious and any resemblance to
real persons, living or dead, is purely coincidental.
All rights reserved. No part of this publication may be reproduced,
stored in a retrieval system, or transmitted, in any form or by any
means, without the prior permission in writing of the publisher, nor
be otherwise circulated in any form of binding or cover other than
that in which it is published and without a similar condition including
this condition being imposed on the subsequent purchaser.

ISBN:1-872889-18-2

ISBN:978-1-872889-18-4

www.isabellamuir.com

Cover photo: by Das Sasha on Unsplash
Cover design: by Christoffer Petersen
Map of Tamarisk Bay: by Richard Whincop

To the peacemakers…

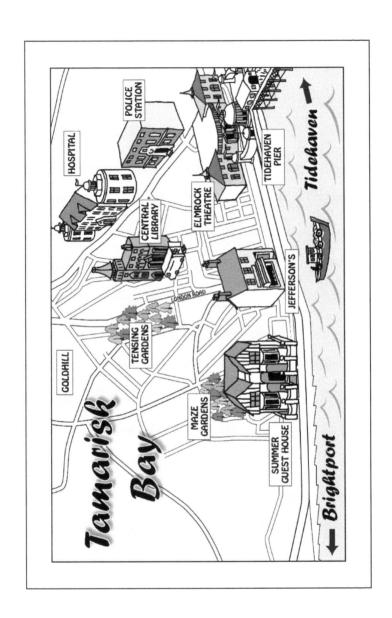

1

The church bells would have rung long and loud. But now there would be no bells, not for Sundays, not for Christmas and not for the missing boy.

The announcement of 3 September changed everything. Now everyone carried a gas mask, although few knew why. Families argued about Christmas. Some said it wasn't right to celebrate it, others said the opposite. Families were fractured and not just in their thoughts on the festivities.

Philip got off his bicycle, leaning it up against the side of the brick outhouse. The last few days had been wet, the bike needed a good clean. Maybe he would tackle it later; right now there were errands to run.

He'd found the best sprigs of holly and mistletoe by pushing the bike through the copse at the back of St Mary's churchyard. As a result, his trousers were covered in mud. His mum would complain, when really he guessed she would be pleased. The scrubbing of clothes, of floors, of anything, all provided distraction from the reality of a war that had crept up on them.

Philip gathered the berry-laden branches from his cycle basket and laid them down on the kitchen hearth. 'What's next?' he asked his mother.

'We've got a few days yet before we need to worry about the tree. That's always been your dad's job.'

'It's okay, I can manage it. I'll drag it if I have to.'

His dad had returned to the same army regiment he'd fought with twenty years before, in the war to end all wars. At least that's what they'd called it. Now what would they say?

'Well there's potatoes and carrots to get. Onions and parsnips too, but it's too early for the sprouts. Besides, there's only so much space in the larder.'

Helen's hands were floury from pastry-making. She brushed a stray hair away from her face, resulting in a white smear on her cheek.

'Jess not helping with the baking?'

'She's upstairs trying to plait her hair. Says now that she's nearly ten she should be able to do it all on her own. There'll be tears at some point, I'm sure.'

'When will you make the mince pies, mum?'

'Same day I always do them. Christmas Eve, just before we set off to mass.'

'They're dad's favourite.'

They shared a glance before she returned to rolling the pastry out on the cold slab of stone that sat to one side of the sink.

'I bet your dad will have a better Christmas dinner than us. Turkey, stuffing and all the trimmings. Don't forget, it's not only us who have sent parcels to the soldiers. Everyone's doing the same.'

'Ronnie's mum says there's talk of rationing.'

'Not before Christmas, surely?' Helen continued to roll out the pastry. She used an empty jam jar to cut out the circles, ready to fill them with the stewed apple she had prepared at first light.

'I'll call in on Ronnie on the way to get the veg then.'

'It's no weather for bike riding. Any more mud on those trousers and I'll have to soak them for a week.'

Philip sidled up to her and put one arm around her waist.

'Away with you. Be back before dark mind. Don't forget about the blackout.'

His favoured route to Ronnie's house took him around the back of Tensing Gardens, through the alleyway and down the steepest hill in Tamarisk Bay. He could build up speed and freewheel down, exhilarated by the sense of danger. Just once he'd missed seeing a stone in the road and ended up flat on his back, black and blue with bruises that took weeks to vanish. The bike hadn't suffered as much as him, just a crooked pedal and a broken chain. But then his dad threatened to sell it.

'Next time it'll be your head that breaks,' he told him, giving him a rough clip round the side of his head that had suffered least in the fall. His mum said very little, just tutting as she bathed his bruises in vinegar water.

'I'll be more careful, promise,' he told them. That was a year ago and since then not one accident. Not even when he and Ronnie raced down the hills side by side, shouting to pedestrians to get out of the way.

He and Ronnie had been friends forever, despite the four years age difference. In fact they were more than friends; Ronnie was the big brother he wished he'd had. And yet it had taken months of persuasion before he could get Ronnie to race. He teased him, told him he'd buy him a yellow jumper.

'Yellow for cowards,' he laughed. When the jokes didn't work, he tried encouragement. 'You won't fall you know and if you do it will only hurt for a bit. But even the bruises are worth it, it's a thrill like no other.'

In the end it was a girl who sealed it. Philomena, with the long plaits and perfect teeth. Her family had moved to Tamarisk Bay a while back and from the first Sunday, when she stood beside her parents in the back pew of St Mary's, the boys couldn't take their eyes off her. She was closer to Ronnie's age than Philip's, but seemed ready to join in the fun when they told her their idea. She promised to kiss the winner of the race and stood at the bottom of Harley Shute, waving and clapping. Neither of the boys was surprised when she ran off as soon as they got off their bikes, ready to claim their prize. But by then Ronnie got the taste for racing, so it was a success of sorts.

Philip parked his bike against the front wall of the Barnards' house. Ronnie kept his bike round the back in the brick-built shed that Mrs Barnard hoped would double up as an air-raid shelter. Although maybe 'hope' was the wrong word.

The back door was always open, the kettle always on the hob. Philip started along the side path towards the back garden when he heard the front door open. Clara Barnard stood on the doorstep beckoning him towards her.

'Is Ronnie up for a ride?' He wheeled his bike from where he'd left it, sitting astride it, ready for his friend to join him.

Clara didn't reply. It was as if the words were trapped in her throat, too scared to emerge.

'He's not with you?' she managed to say, after a pause.

'I've been on errands for mum, but I told him I'd be over this afternoon.'

'He left first thing. No breakfast, up and out while it was still dark.' She held her hands out towards Philip, hoping he would deliver her son into them. Returning him to the fold.

'Early to work then? I thought this was his day off.'

'He left early this morning,' she repeated, as though she was trying to remember the sequence of events.

'On his bike?' Philip got off his bike, turning it around

4

to wheel it down the path at the side of the house that led to the back garden. Clara followed, her mule slippers flipping and flopping as she walked. She caught the edge of a puddle, one slipper was soaked with dirty rainwater.

Philip wanted to tell her to wait, to go back inside, into the warm and dry. But his words would be wasted. Clara Barnard was looking for her son. He wasn't in the house, in the warm and dry.

'His bike is here, he doesn't go anywhere without his bike,' she said, staring at the bike, which was parked in its regular spot in the shed.

'Perhaps there's a puncture?' There was a practical answer Philip was certain. He turned towards Clara at the same moment she turned away from him. She muttered something, words he couldn't catch.

'Pardon?'

'You need to find him, Philip. You need to find Ronnie.'

'Didn't he say anything? Not where he was going or why so early?'

'He didn't even have breakfast,' she said, shaking her head as if she couldn't grasp the meaning of her own words.

'I'll find him, Mrs Barnard, don't you worry.'

Philip knew that worry was there, around the edge of all the words – his and hers.

'It's nearly Christmas. I need him here.'

It was an hour until blackout. An hour for Philip to find his friend, to bring him home. There were places they would go to, to sneak a cigarette, even a can of beer. Fortune Park was one. Years ago they had made a camp there, at the far end of the park, among some of the trees and bushes. Now, they were both too old for such childish things; Ronnie had just turned eighteen, he was a man. And even though Philip was four years his junior he felt like a man too, now that he was done with school and had just started work with the Royal Mail.

The viaduct over the back of the recreation ground was another of their favourite places. Then there was the riverbank. Ronnie had taught Philip to fish, teaching himself at the same time.

The bag with Philip's gas mask clanked against the handlebars as he cycled towards Fortune Park. His plan was to start at the furthest place and then work back, leaving the viaduct until last. He could do the whole route in just under an hour and be home before blackout.

The news reports warned that 4,000 people had been killed on the roads since the start of the war. In just four months. December days meant darkness fell early, people were coming home from work in the dark, cars had to drive without lights. Casualties were inevitable.

Philip's work was just around the corner from home. But Ronnie worked in Marley's Butchers, half an hour's walk from the Barnards' house, less than ten minutes on the bike. Five if you knew your way in the dark.

A week before Christmas the butcher's shop would be busy. That was it. Why didn't he think of it before? Why hadn't Mrs Barnard thought of it? Even though Wednesday was Ronnie's usual day off, he must have gone in to work to help out with the pre-Christmas rush.

Philip altered his route back from Fortune Park, ignoring the riverbank and headed straight to Marley's Butchers. There were no lights in the shop window, the closed sign was hanging inside the front door. Mr Marley lived above the shop. If he and Ronnie were working out the back, then Mrs Marley would know.

Philip dropped his bike on the pavement in front of the shop and ran up the iron staircase to the Marley's front door.

'What is it, lad?' Mr Marley was old, his hearing wasn't as sharp as it used to be and as a consequence he shouted. Perhaps it helped him to hear his own voice.

'Is Ronnie with you?' Philip enunciated clearly.

Then Mrs Marley appeared behind her husband. 'What's all the shouting?'

'I'm sorry, but I'm just trying to track down Ronnie. I thought he might be with you at the shop?'

Philip didn't need to hear the answer; Ronnie wasn't at work.

'I'm sorry to disturb you.' He returned to his bike while Mr and Mrs Marley stood together on the little iron landing outside their front door. As he rode away Mr Marley called out, 'Tell him not to be late in the morning, we've a busy few days ahead. Folk still want their Christmas dinner, you know. War or no war.'

There was about twenty minutes left of daylight. Although it couldn't be described as light, more of a murky grey; that halfway house between day and night. They had just had the winter equinox. The shortest day and the longest night.

There wasn't time now to reach the viaduct and anyway, why would Ronnie be there on a cold December day, on his own for hours, without his bike?

Leaning his bike against the outhouse again he pushed the back door open. His mum was bending over, peering into the oven, the blast of heat bringing a flush to her cheeks. The cheeks that were still smudged with flour. She didn't need to look at her son. She knew him well enough to recognise this breathing, usually so slow and steady, now coming in gasps.

'Ronnie?' she said.

'He's gone, mum.'

'Gone where?'

'I don't know.'

2

Thursday would be busy. The Royal Mail had to sort just as many letters and parcels as they had last Christmas and the Christmas before that. It didn't matter what Britain had told Hitler. People still wanted to post Christmas cards and presents, to send festive cheer to family and friends who needed it now more than ever.

Philip would be there from early morning until late afternoon, checking addresses and filling the cubby holes of the wooden shelving that covered one wall of the sorting office. He knew all the roads in Tamarisk Bay, most of the names on the envelopes too. These were friends he'd gone to school with, families his parents invited round for tea and cake on warm summer afternoons. But now there were letters coming from the Front. Foreign postmarks with messages of hope inside. Hope that soon the fighting would be over and the men would return home. Before Christmas? Probably not.

He stopped for a mid-morning tea break. As he opened his flask and poured the stewed tea into the plastic mug, he was certain Ronnie was doing the same. He would be at Marley's now. Maybe he would be forcing sausagemeat through the mincer, or chopping the chicken into thighs, or legs, or breasts. Since Ronnie had started work he'd learned an impressive range of butchery skills from old Mr Marley. He knew the best cuts of meat, how long to cook the cheapest ones so they would be soft and tender. At first Ronnie had to cope with plenty of teasing. Philip warned him not to chop his hand off, or put his fingers through the mincer. It got so that Ronnie almost didn't go that first day. But when Philip called round to his friend's house that Monday evening, Ronnie waved his hands in front of him.

'Look, still got all my fingers and not a slice in sight.'

They laughed as they compared notes. When Philip left school and joined the Royal Mail Ronnie got his own back. 'You'll be stamping your hand,' he joked.

'No chance.'

'Or paper cuts. Maybe you'd better get yourself a job in the butcher's instead.'

They shared most things; cycle rides, choir practice, fishing, even the dreams they had about Philomena. Now his friend had gone off without telling him, it didn't make any sense. He needed to call back round to Ronnie's tonight to make sure he was home, but his mum was worried about the blackout.

The sirens had sounded a couple of times over the last few weeks. It terrified everyone, until they discovered they were practice runs.

'If the sirens go when you're out in the street, you know what to do, don't you?' His mum's voice rose in pitch when she was anxious. Several places throughout the town had been designated as safe shelters. Although how safe anywhere would be if a bomb landed was anyone's guess.

Philip decided to take a risk. He cycled to Ronnie's straight after work and let himself in the back door. The kitchen table was laid for tea.

'Where is everyone? Where's that wandering friend of mine? You gave us a bit of a fright you know.' He was talking as he walked down the hallway towards the sound of voices. The sitting room door was open just a crack; he pushed it further open to reveal several members of the Barnard family. But no Ronnie.

Mrs Barnard was kneeling on the floor next to the coal fire, with a bowl of water beside her and Gracie on her lap.

'I've been helping,' Gracie said, holding up chubby hands covered in treacle.

'Be still a minute. I need to wipe your face too. How much of that treacle went into your tummy and not the cake?'

'Do you know where Ronnie is?' Gracie said, struggling to be free of her mother.

'He didn't come home last night? I thought he'd be at work today. I was certain of it.'

Now that Gracie's hands and face were clean she pulled away from Clara and plonked herself in-between the two children who were sitting quietly on the settee.

'These are vacuees,' Gracie said proudly.

'Evacuees,' Clara Barnard said, getting to her feet and lifting the bowl carefully to avoid spilling it.

'Here, let me take that.' Philip followed her out to the kitchen and watched her empty the water down the sink. She dried her hands on a tea towel, then brought the tea towel to her face. When she turned back to Philip he could see she'd been crying.

'I don't know what to do. I have to be here for Gracie and those other poor mites. They don't know what's going on. First they leave their family behind, sent to live with strangers, then just when we're trying to settle together, get used to be a family of sorts…'

'They're good kids?'

'I keep thinking how it would be for Gracie if they sent her away. At Christmas too.'

'It was good of you to take them both.'

'Brother and sister can't be apart. It's not right.' She filled the kettle and put it back on the hob.

'You'll stay for tea?'

Philip shook his head. 'I've promised mum. She worries. What with the blackout and the sirens.'

'I don't know what to do, Philip.'

'If Mr Barnard was here, what would he do?'

He'd always been a little afraid of Ronnie's dad, with his monosyllabic grunts, bald head and beady eyes that peered at him through wire-framed specs. Philip made unfair comparisons with his own dad, a man whose thick crop of hair on his head was matched by the depth of love in his heart.

'Makes no difference what he would do,' Clara replied. 'He's fighting his own battles, there won't be time for him to think of us.'

While they were talking the children had come into the kitchen, led by Gracie. She was the youngest and yet clearly in charge. It was her home, after all.

'Bobby doesn't like jam,' Gracie announced. 'He likes mamade.'

'Marmalade,' the young boy said. It was the first time Philip had heard him speak. No surprise that Bobby and his sister, Jemima, had lost their voices. They had already lost everything else. London may only be fifty miles away, but it might as well be on the other side of the world.

Clara cut the loaf into thick slices, buttered them and put two slices on each of the children's plates. 'Make the most. There's talk of butter rationing in the new year.'

She turned to Philip and gestured to him to follow her. As the two of them climbed the steep staircase to the upstairs landing Philip could hear all three children giggling. The evacuees had found their voices and laughter was the result. Perhaps the day was not a complete disaster.

He followed Clara into Ronnie's bedroom. First she opened his wardrobe, tugging at the door that was warped and twisted with age. She said nothing, but pointed at two empty wooden hangers. Next she went to his tallboy, opening each drawer, running her hand over the folded shirts, the neatly paired socks.

And then she spoke. 'I've counted what he's taken. It's enough for five days. That's if he changes his socks and underpants every two days. He like to be clean, does our Ronnie.' Her tone was defiant. Her son had taken what he needed for five days and then he'd come for Christmas. She sat on Ronnie's bed, smoothing out the creases in the blankets.

'We need to find him, Philip. You're his best friend, you know where he'd go to. Help me to find him.'

'What about money?'

'He'll have his wages from Marley's. He gives me money for rent and food, but he'll have some put by.'

'Enough?' Philip didn't want to think about the distance that his friend's savings could buy him. Bus tickets, train tickets. It would be an impossible search. 'Should we tell the police?' He knew the answer before he asked the question.

Mrs Barnard shook her head.

'I'll ask for a day off. I'll go into work tomorrow and explain. Then I can look in daylight. It's our best bet.'

'They won't let you take time off. This will be your busiest week. All those cards and parcels.'

She tucked her hand into her apron pocket, pulled out an envelope and handed it to Philip. He looked at her for confirmation that he should open it and read the contents.

'Go ahead. It's from Ronnie's dad. He doesn't say much, or at least once they've cut out half the words there's not much left to read.'

Philip glanced through the short letter that looked as though it had been written in a hurry.

'He's grateful for the socks,' he said. 'If they've got the cold and wet that we've got here, then at least his feet will be warm and dry inside his boots.'

He wanted to put a hand on her hand, or on her shoulder. A touch to let her know she wasn't alone. Instead his hand hovered in mid-air, before finding its way into his pocket.

'I'll take a sick day.' Philip walked towards the door. 'I must go. Mum will have my guts for garters.'

'You're a good lad. A good friend to Ronnie.'

'Try not to worry, Mrs Barnard.'

She was still sitting on Ronnie's bed when he went back along the landing and downstairs into the kitchen. A brief glance at Gracie's face confirmed that much of the jam had missed her mouth. Some had even found its way to the tip of her nose.

All three children had empty plates and were now playing *I spy*, taking it in turns to cover their eyes when calling out their guesses. It seemed they were mixing up *Blind man's buff* with the guessing game, but regardless of the rules they were having fun.

'Maybe help Mrs Barnard by clearing the table.' He directed his words to Jemima. He guessed she was around eight or nine; a good age to learn about domestic chores. She slid off her chair and began stacking the plates, pointing towards the dirty cutlery that had been left in a pile in the centre of the table. Gracie followed suit, seeing a chance to dip her hands into soapy water, which would surely mean bubbles that could be blown around the kitchen.

'Your mum needs you to be a good girl, Gracie. She's got other things to worry about and can't be worrying about you,' Philip said, just as Mrs Barnard came into the kitchen.

Gracie responded by putting a wet hand into her skirt pocket, pulling out a piece of bread that had been folded in two. The jam that she had spread liberally over it was now oozing out over her skirt, her hands, dripping onto the floor.

'Oh, Gracie, now what have you done,' her mother shrieked.

'I'm saving it for Ronnie. He'll be hungry when he gets home.'

3

Several people in the town had received their call-up papers. Helen Chandler remembered the last time. Her husband, George, had been an army cadet, so once the announcement was made in 1914 he'd been allocated to a regiment and sent off to the front.

Philip knew a little about that war, a war that was fought in the mud, in the trenches.

'Don't ask,' his mum had told him when he was old enough to understand. 'It's enough that he came back to us in one piece. Millions didn't.

The occasional visits to the cemetery were a reminder about the fragility of life. But the dead soldiers weren't in St Mary's cemetery or in any other cemetery in Tamarisk Bay. They were laying in foreign fields, many in unmarked graves.

Philip had been born during those years of normality, when husband and wife learned how it was to be joined together again when so much had been broken around them.

A week or so ago Philip dropped round to pick up his friend for their weekly bike ride and noticed the letter on Ronnie's mantelpiece, propped up between a brass candlestick and a china ornament. Mrs Barnard loved her china ornaments; they were scattered over most of the downstairs surfaces. A few were Toby jugs, but most were cats; sitting, laying, or curled up, with that supercilious expression that cats do so well.

'You've not opened it yet?' he asked his friend. If the letter was Philip's he would have torn it open the minute it arrived. It would be an adventure of sorts, a chance to see another country, maybe two.

'Are we going for that bike ride, or what?' Ronnie's impatience took Philip by surprise.

'Open it first. See where they're going to send you.'

His friend threw his jacket over his arm and walked through to the kitchen, leaving Philip to follow.

'Cycle clips?' Clara Barnard stood with the metal clips in her hand holding them out towards her son.

'Don't need them, the ground is dry enough. It's a few days since we had rain. He kicked at the bottom of the back door and it flung open. 'I'll be back for tea,' he called out over his shoulder, as he retreated down the path towards the shed.

Ronnie led for most of their ride that day. They made their way up to the railway viaduct, down through the valley and along the river bank. Several times Philip called for him to stop, but Ronnie had no plans to stop. When you're riding you can't answer questions.

'Well, I'm stopping for a bit, even if you're not.' Philip braked too hard, his front wheel slid and threw him off balance. He landed abruptly on the edge of the footpath that ran alongside the riverbank. Ronnie slowed up and turned to see his friend flat on his rump.

'Alright?'

'Bit bruised, nothing broken.'

'How about the bike?'

'All in one piece, a bit of luck I reckon.'

Ronnie pulled Philip to his feet and they both wheeled their bikes along the path a few paces to a nearby bench.

'I'll just have a breather.' Philip lowered his bike on the ground and watched his friend do the same.

'What's the rush today, Ron?'

Ronnie shrugged. It was hard to find the right words. After a few minutes silence he took a deep breath. 'I'm not a murderer.'

Philip's first reaction was to laugh. His friend must have been reading too many crime novels.

'Tell me something I don't know.'

'If I go to war, I'll have to fight, maybe kill. I can't do that.'

Now Philip understood the reason for the unopened letter.

'You can't avoid it, Ronnie, everyone has to go.'

Back then, on that bike ride, with the call-up letter sitting unopened on the mantelpiece of the Barnards' house, Philip couldn't guess that it would lead to something else. Something else so frightening that his friend could go to prison. Mrs Barnard knew it though. She knew why her son had run away. She knew the police couldn't be the ones to find him.

Helen Chandler couldn't give her blessing for her son to take a sick day when he wasn't sick. It was wrong. But Philip's friend was in trouble. Sometimes rules had to be broken, but no-one would hear her admit it.

Jessica thought sneaking a day off was an excellent idea. She wished Phil would do it more often, especially now she was on school holidays. They might have been a few years apart in age, but they'd shared secrets since they were old enough to conjure them up.

'It's one day, mum,' Jessica used her most grown-up voice. 'Besides, Phil might be the only person who can find Ronnie. He knows all his favourite places. Plus it's nearly Christmas, so nothing bad is allowed to happen.'

'You're not a child anymore, Jessica. Life doesn't always give us fairytale endings.'

But Jessica wasn't listening. She had wrapped a woollen scarf tightly around her neck, grabbed her gloves and was heading out the back door. She would make her own plans. Adults were confusing. One minute they were telling you to grow up, the next that you were young to understand.

'That girl lives in a dream world. She'll struggle when it comes to hard work, I'm sure of it.' But Helen was talking to herself. Philip had left. He'd rode off on his bike, with a flask of hot tea and some digestive biscuits tucked inside the bag he'd slung over the handlebars.

By the time he reached the end of the footpath he'd moved the bag, slinging it over his shoulder instead. Broken biscuits were one thing, a broken flask quite another.

As he cycled he replayed conversations he'd had with Ronnie over recent days. The ones where Ronnie had shouted, told him it wasn't about being a coward.

'I know you think it's because I'm scared. You've always thought that,' his friend said.

'That's not true, Ron. It was only ever teasing. I've never meant anything by it.'

'Well, I'm not scared. I know I might get killed, or lose a leg or an arm. I've thought about all of it. How it will be for mum, for Gracie. And if dad doesn't make it through this war, then it will be even harder for them with no man around to help.'

'You can't think like that. Your dad, my dad, they both made it through the first war. There's no reason we won't all make it through this one.'

'You're not listening to me.'

They were taking a breather in part of the wooded area of Fortune Park. Ronnie stood beside one of the tall oaks and beat a fist against the gnarled trunk. 'That's not the reason. It's not about being hurt. It's about the other bloke.'

'The Nazi? You're worried about killing a Nazi?'

'The German soldiers, they're just like us. They have families, brothers, sisters, friends. Someone has to say 'No'. If we all said 'No', then maybe there wouldn't be a war.'

'We'll just let Hitler walk through France, take his troops across the English Channel and occupy our towns and villages, shall we?' Philip could feel his blood rising, his heart was beating fast.

'You won't change my mind.'

They cycled back home that day and Philip spent a few nights tossing and turning, struggling to settle the argument in his mind. He didn't dare talk to his mum about it and this time even Jess had to be kept out of it. Not that she would really understand. This was about the law. Philip knew that if his friend refused to fight he could end up in prison.

The last Sunday bike ride they had together before Ronnie's disappearance, Philip had prepared his argument. He'd worked out what he would say to his friend to make him see sense.

'Didn't hear you singing in church this morning.' They had reached the half-way point of their ride and had stopped for a breather.

'Wasn't in the mood for singing.'

'All I could hear was old Jack Tarby. Tone deaf and thinks he's still a choir boy. Kind of spoilt the singing altogether, don't you think?'

Ronnie shrugged. Singing hymns in tune or out of tune was so far down his list of concerns he didn't even have an opinion.

'And that's the point, do you see?' Philip said.

'What?'

'Well, it's only when everyone pulls together that things work out right. You not singing spoiled the service for the rest of us.'

'What are you on about singing for?'

'If you don't fight, then you'll be letting your country down. And me too.'

'I'm not fighting, Phil, and you'd better get used to the idea.'

'What about your mum and Gracie?'

'That's just it. I need to be here to look out for them.'

'The whole town will be against you and against them. Once it gets out you're a consci there'll be those who want to make your life a misery, shove dirt through your letterbox, paint bad words on your front wall. You can't let your mum and Gracie go through that.'

Perhaps it was Philip's argument that tipped the scales. But if it was, then it tipped them in the wrong direction. Ronnie hadn't said any more that day. Instead he made a plan; this disappearing act was his answer. It must be the only way he could see to stay true to his beliefs, but still protect his mum and little sister.

There was only one other place Philip could think of that Ronnie might choose to hide. St Clement's Caves. They had been there together a few times in the school summer holidays. Philip had joked about them being haunted, scaring himself more than he cared to admit. It was true enough that people talked of hauntings by the smugglers of long ago. The caves lay deep beneath the ruins of Tidehaven Castle. It was ironic that there was little left of the castle, bar a few broken walls and piles of stones, but the caves were intact, just as they would have been in smugglers' days.

Philip dismounted his bike at the foot of the West Hill and made the steady climb up the steps towards the caves. The cliff railway had been out of action since war was declared, but even if it had been working he couldn't have taken his bike into the little cable car. His mum and dad had taken him and Jessica on the little railway several times as a special treat. It took just a few minutes for the single carriage of the narrow funicular railway to climb the steep face of the cliff and once they reached the top he wished he could linger for a while to take in the whole expanse of the seafront, the Old Town and the tall, wooden fishing huts. Instead, his dad would hurry them up and after a brisk walk over the clifftop they would head back down again, but this time via the steps, all one hundred and fifty of them.

At the mouth of the caves he stopped and laid his bike against a rock. He cupped his hands around his mouth and called out, 'Ronnie'. His voice was blown away on the fierce wind that he'd been fighting against all the way over to Tidehaven. He tried again, louder this time. 'Ronnie, are you there?'

He had brought his dad's torch. He pushed the switch and directed the light into the heart of the first cave. The network of caves ran through the hill. Ronnie could be deep inside. He would have to venture further in. He walked forward, trying to watch his footing, while at the same time looking ahead, in the direction of the torchlight.

And then he heard a sound.

4

'Ronnie, is that you?' His voice echoed back at him as he made his way deeper into the caves.

The stillness of the air made the cold more intense. He directed the torch to the left, then to the right, but the light merely showed the blank rock walls. The cave nearest the entrance was the wettest, with moisture trickling down the walls to form puddles on the ground. Some of the puddles joined together to create a rivulet, running down towards the interior of the rocky network.

There was no path as such, just large and small boulders to pick his way across. Sometimes he had to stuff the torch in his pocket to leave both hands free to negotiate the best route. Without the light the darkness was oppressive, making it feel that the walls were closer to him, the roof of the cave bearing down. In reality, the roof was maybe a foot or so above him in most places, so he could stand straight without fear of banging his head.

He heard the noise again and stood still for a moment to focus his mind, to try to determine what the sound was and which direction it came from. He took a few paces further forward and shone the touch directly ahead, doing a sweep from roof to ground.

Perhaps it was the light that disturbed them, or maybe it was the sudden intrusion of a human being, for in the next moment two rats ran out from one side of the cave and headed towards him.

'Oh dear God,' he shouted, dropped his torch and stepped abruptly to one side. But as he moved he twisted his foot, something gave way in his right ankle and he was on the ground. 'Jesus, not now, please.'

The patch of ground he'd fallen onto was dry, but he was fairly certain the torch had fallen into the small stream that edged the cave. He had heard the splash of water at the same moment that the torchlight was extinguished. He slid one hand carefully across the ground towards the water, terrified that it wouldn't be the torch he would find, but a rat.

In order to reach further along the ground he would have to move. He tried to move his right leg, leaning on one hand to provide some leverage. At worst he had broken his ankle. At best it was a severe sprain. Either way, the only way he could move now was to crawl.

'Ronnie, wherever you are, now's the time to say a prayer or two.'

They had both traipsed along to church every Sunday since as far back as he could remember. Their families weren't fiercely religious, but church on Sunday was as commonplace as the Sunday roast. It was the same for most folk in Tamarisk Bay. So much so that families had their regular pews. There was a comfort in knowing that at 9am every Sunday, the Chandler family would be lined up along the third pew back from the altar and right behind them would be the Barnard family. Everyone spruced up in their Sunday best.

Never once had the boys spoken about their beliefs. In truth, Philip had never given it much thought. But right at this moment he hoped there was a God and that he would lend a hand to get him out of these blessed caves before he froze to death.

Perhaps it was the shock, or the pain, or the fear of the rats, but whatever the reason, he started to shiver and didn't seem able to stop. Now that he was on the ground and not moving the intensity of the cold and damp filtered through his jacket and jeans. He'd never been one for gloves or scarves or hats, but now he craved them all. Anything to stop the shivering. The flask of hot tea and the digestive biscuits offered no comfort; he had left them in the bag that was hanging on the handlebars of his bicycle.

He edged forwards on his hands and knees, moving one hand through the water until he located the torch. He grabbed it, dried it off on his jacket and willed it to work. There was a chance that the water had got into it, or the bulb could have broken when he dropped it. A positive rush of adrenalin flowed through him as he flicked the switch and the torchlight altered the fearful blackness into a murky half-light.

He moved position slightly and once again tried to put a little weight on his right leg, testing it to see if he could stand the pain for long enough to get him back to the mouth of the cave. From there, surely, he could get help. But there was no strength in his ankle, it would never hold him up.

He raised himself to standing, wondering if he could hop on his one good leg, steadying himself by holding onto the cave walls. He took one hop forward, only to land on the ground again, this time banging one knee against a boulder. The ground was too uneven for hopping. He would have to crawl out, it was the only safe way. It didn't matter how long it took, slow progress might be less risky.

Helen Chandler filled the kettle again. Clara had arrived a little after Philip left and since then several cups of tea had been drunk. Gracie, Bobby and Jemima had been plied with milk and biscuits before being shooed out into the back garden, where Gracie was organising a game of hide and seek.

'She's a character, your little girl,' Helen said. 'Not much will get past her when she's grown.'

'Trouble is she think she's grown already.' Clara sipped her tea, while standing at the kitchen sink to keep her eye on the children.

'Are they much trouble?'

'The evacuees? No, none at all. Although the first few nights we had wet sheets, which didn't surprise me. Can't say I'd cope well myself if I was sent to live with strangers, even at my age, let alone as a young'un.'

'We're due to take one when the next lot arrive. If it's a boy he'll share with Philip, if not then Jessica's room has just enough space for another bed. Although it'll be a bit of a squeeze.'

'Where is Jessica this morning?'

'She spends her days round her friend's house given the chance. I think the girls spend most of the time in Lucy's bedroom doing each other's hair. If Jess ends up as a hairdresser I pity her customers. She'd be just as likely to give a perm to someone who wants their curls cut off. She's such a dreamer, I hope Lucy's mother won't get fed up with her.'

'It's so good of your Philip to go searching for Ronnie. Will he get into trouble for taking a sick day, with Christmas just days away. They won't be happy with him.'

Helen waved her hand to dismiss the idea, then added more water to the teapot. 'Is it stewed? Shall I make fresh?'

'When do you think he'll be back?'

'Philip?'

'Yes, I don't want to impose, but I'd like to be here. To hear first-hand how he got on.'

'You must stay for lunch. I'll make soup. You can help if you like.'

26

Helen went to the larder and filled a colander with carrots, onions and potatoes, tipping them into the sink to wash.

'Do you know why Ronnie has gone?' Helen focused on peeling and chopping the vegetables. 'You don't need to say if you'd rather not.'

Clara took her cup to the sink, emptied it and ran some cold water through it. 'I think I know, but I can't be certain. He's got his own way of thinking has Ronnie. Always been the same, since he was little.'

'That can be a good thing.'

'Some folk won't agree. If you have your own opinion then you stand out from the crowd and people don't like that. It makes them feel uncomfortable.'

While the soup was being prepared Helen cut up a loaf and laid five places at the kitchen table.

'I'll get those children in now, they'll need to get their hands washed before we eat.'

She stepped out into the back garden and felt something land on her face. She looked up to the sky to see snowflakes falling; at first slow and delicate, but within minutes they were coming down so thick and fast they covered the path ahead of her.

'Children, come on in now. We're having hot soup and looks like we'll be needing it.'

The anticipation of snowball fights and the building of snowmen far outweighed any attraction offered by a hot bowl of soup. But Clara wasn't taking no for an answer. 'You can come back out after we've eaten, but only if you promise to eat what you're given.'

'I don't like onions,' Gracie announced as she walked into the kitchen.

27

'Stand still all of you.' The two mothers peeled wet coats from the children and made them stamp their shoes clean on the doormat.

By the time the last piece of bread had been dunked and the soup bowls were emptied, the back garden was no longer green. A blanket of fresh white snowflakes covered the paths, the grass, the hedge and the solitary apple tree that a few months earlier had provided the filling for dozens of pies.

'There's more to come, the sky is full of it,' Helen said, looking out of the window as she ran hot water into the sink.

'Then the weather will be the only thing that's right about this Christmas. Your husband and mine both off fighting, folk scared to leave their homes after dark. Even scared in the daylight with the threat of bombs or worse.'

She took one of the gas masks from the kitchen dresser and thumped it down on the table. 'Doesn't take much imagination to work out why we need these. You know what the gas attacks did to those poor souls in the Great War. Doesn't lead us to think much of Christmas cheer.' Her face was flushed now, despite the cold draught that filtered under the back door as a result of the old warped timber.

'Can we go out now?' Gracie appeared, holding hands with Jemima, and Bobby bringing up the rear. They had been in the sitting room, whispering about Santa Claus, hoping the grown-ups would start talking about important things like presents, rather than bombs and gas masks.

Helen went to the understairs cupboard, picking two of Jessica's woollen scarves from one of the coat hooks. She wrapped one around Gracie's head, looping the long end around her neck. The other she handed to Jemima.

'Will you be warm enough, Bobby?' The boy had barely said two words since he arrived, but seemed content to follow his sister and her new bossy friend.

'Will Ronnie come home for tea?' Gracie said, as Clara eased her arms into her coat, the action being made more difficult because Gracie was struggling to stand still.

'Go and play and don't get too cold. When you can't feel your fingers anymore it's time to come in. Do you hear me?'

Helen and Clara cleared the rest of the lunch things and tried to avoid looking at the kitchen clock, or at the snow that continued to fall.

'Will you have a tree?' Clara asked after a period of silence when they were both immersed in their own thoughts.

'George always gets the tree. Without him here it doesn't seem right to be celebrating.'

'Gracie's so little. It's not fair on her if I don't at least make an effort. She keeps asking when she can write her letter to Santa. Last year we let her put it on the fire and told her it went up the chimney and Santa would be there to read it at the other end. It's all she's worried about.'

'Be nice to have worries like that.'

It wasn't dark yet, but Helen liked to draw the blackout curtains closed early, taking time to cover any gaps with brown paper. They had been practising what to do in the blackout for months before war was declared. The government had even issued a leaflet telling them not to wash the curtains, it seemed that it would make them apt to let in more light. Instead, 'hoover, shake, brush, then iron' was the advice. Maybe it was all a ruse to distract folk from worrying about the real reason that whole towns and villages had to disappear once the sun set.

'If Ronnie doesn't come home I don't know what I'll do.' Clara plopped herself down onto one of the kitchen chairs with such a thud it startled Helen. She turned away from the sink to see her friend with her hands covering her face. She could hear from the way she was breathing that she was trying to control the sobs that were threatening to overwhelm her.

'Philip will bring him home. I'm certain of it. I've told him to make sure he's back before dark, so anytime now the two of them will walk through the door together and they'll be wondering what all the fuss is about.'

5

Philip's progress was slow and painful. The distance he had covered in half an hour on foot when going into the caves was taking him three times as long to do on his hands and knees. He'd found the best approach was to keep the torch in his right hand and use his left to feel ahead a little so that when he moved each knee he could make sure he placed it squarely on a flat piece of ground. Occasionally he had no choice but to kneel on a rock or boulder; his knees and shins were so bruised now that another knock or scratch made little difference.

As he made his way slowly forward he tried to concentrate on the next stage. Once he was out of the caves he would have to get home somehow. He had left his bike outside the cave entrance, but there was no way he'd be able to ride home. Freewheeling down the hills might be doable, but he would have no way of gaining momentum along the flat. Plus the descent from the caves involved those steps again.

He was mad with himself that he hadn't told his mum where he was headed. He'd planned the route for his search, but hadn't bothered sharing it with anyone. Not even Jessica. It would mean that no-one would be looking for him. Or at least if they did look they wouldn't know where to go. Pretty much the same as his search for Ronnie.

For the first time Philip considered the possibility that Ronnie might be lying injured somewhere. Until now he had just assumed he'd chosen to disappear; anything to avoid having to fight. But maybe Ronnie had had an accident and was just waiting and hoping someone would find him.

His thoughts spurred him on. He sensed he was nearing the cave entrance. There was a change in the light. Philip couldn't work out what it was. It was as if the torch was burning brighter somehow. He stopped moving and turned the torch off. He reached a bend; he remembered it from when he had made his way in. He crawled forward a little so that he could see around the curve of the cave wall.

He took a moment for his eyes to focus, such was the difference between the gloom of the journey he had made to this point and the shining brightness of the fresh snowfall that filled his vision.

The snow had blown a little way into the entrance of the cave where it created an icy lip. He stopped just short of the entrance and looked out across the hill. What was green and mud and pathway a few hours earlier was now a pristine carpet of white. The snow was still falling steadily, the flakes swirling around as they were caught by the brisk northerly wind that had been there since daybreak.

The north wind shall blow and we shall have snow...

Philip smiled at the memory of the nursery rhyme. But the smile faded quickly when he pulled himself out of the cave. His plan was to use his bike as a crutch, then maybe he would have had a chance of making it home. But the bike wasn't there. Two miles was nothing to cycle, even to walk, if both legs were working. But two miles of crawling or hopping on ground that was covered with inches of snow would be near on impossible. And soon it would be dark. The only good thing about the snow at night would be the light it offered, a helpful reflection of a clear moonlit sky.

Philip tucked the torch into his jacket pocket, swung his legs round to move from kneeling to sitting and then he heard a sound. This time he was certain it wasn't rats, or any other kind of animal. It was a sharp whistle, not a bird's tuneful song, but the whistle of a man calling his sheepdog. Before Philip had a chance to work out which direction the sound was coming from the sheepdog appeared beside him, tail wagging, beating away the snow as it fell.

'Hello, can you help me?' Philip called out across the empty hillside.

The dog sniffed around Philip for a few seconds then ran off again. He was running so fast that within a few moments he was out of Philip's sight, over the brow of the hill. Then, out of his peripheral vision he saw a man padding across the snow, lifting each boot and placing it down purposefully. Scared that dog and owner would take another route and miss him altogether, he called out again.

'I'm over here by the caves. I need help.'

The man's approach was silenced by the snow. As he got closer Philip could see that the man was maybe seventy or more, his shoulders pushed forward towards the approaching wind. The curve of his back made him stoop a little and he carried a walking stick, which he was using to brush away the drifting snow ahead of his feet. Philip envied him his heavy overcoat and the thick scarf that was wrapped his neck. Although the shivering had stopped once he started moving through the caves, his fingers and toes didn't feel as though they belonged to him anymore.

The man reached Philip and bent down towards him, offering a hand.

'Need a lift up, lad?'

'No. I mean, yes, but I've done something to my ankle. I can't put any weight on it.'

'Here on your own?'

'Yes, I was looking for a friend. He's gone missing.'

'Not meeting your sweetheart then?' The man chuckled. 'These caves haven't only been used for smuggling, you know. I could tell you some tales.'

'Could you help me to stand?'

'Here, pull on my arm.' He placed his right arm out towards Philip, bending it and holding it firm. He moved his feet apart slightly to create a steady base and then told Philip he was ready.

'I don't want to pull you over.'

'I'm tougher than I look. You pull away, I'll not let you down.'

Philip tugged on the man's arm and pulled himself up to stand on his left leg, avoiding the temptation to put any weight on his damaged ankle.

'Now you're upright take a hold of this stick, it'll steady you. What's your name, lad?'

'Philip Chandler.'

'And I'm Joseph Christmas. A good name for this time of year, eh?' he chuckled to himself as between them they moved a few slow paces away from the cave entrance.

'Wait,' Philip said.

'What is it, lad?'

'My bike, I need to find it. I left it just here when I went into the cave.' He pointed towards a high drift of snow that had settled against the outside wall of the caves.

'I'm going to let go of you for a minute. Just stand right there, I don't want you falling over.'

Joseph turned his back on Philip and walked over to the snow drift. He whistled for his dog who had been scurrying around. The snow hadn't just covered the ground, it had blanketed out all the interesting smells of rabbits, hares and squirrels. Joseph signalled to his dog, making a movement with his hand. The dog began to dig at the base of the snow drift, working his way forward as the soft snow fell behind him and over him. Philip and Joseph watched and waited. Joseph with a confidence that his dog would achieve the task with ease, Philip with a fascination as to the dog's motivation. He'd never owned a dog but now, seeing the energy and skill with which the dog fulfilled his master's commands, he wished he had his own dog, just like this one.

Within a few minutes the result of the digging was apparent. First a tyre and then the pedals and chain emerged from the winter blanket. Joseph stepped forward, caressed the dog's ears and signalled for him to stop digging and move back. A few seconds later Joseph had pulled the bike clear of the snow that had piled on top of it. He moved the bike towards Philip, offering it as a crutch for him to lean on.

'Clever dog,' Philip said, partly to Joseph and partly to the dog who now stood in front of him, tail wagging. 'He deserves a treat.'

Joseph made a clicking sound, dug one hand into his coat pocket and when the dog sat he was rewarded with a handful of biscuits.

'We've got to get you home, lad. Where do you live?'

The scene would have made an amusing painting; a snowy hillside, a young boy, leaning on a bicycle to one side and an elderly man to the other, and the sheepdog crisscrossing beside and around them.

'Do you know the history of the caves?' Joseph said as they walked.

'Not really. Ronnie and I used to hang around them in the summer holidays, daring each other as to who would go in the furthest.'

'The story is that a couple were thrown out of the workhouse back in the seventeen hundreds. Seems they'd misbehaved. Folk said they went to live in these caves, died there too, I expect.'

Philip didn't want to think about dying in such a bleak place.

'What about your friend?' Joseph's voice brought him back.

'He doesn't like the idea of war.'

'None of us do, lad.'

'He's refusing to join up. I think that's why he's run away.'

Joseph nodded, as though he was having a conversation with someone, offering voiceless answers to silent questions.

'Did you fight in the Great War, Joseph?'

'Nothing great about it. Watching your friends and comrades being blown to pieces around you, wondering why them and not you.'

'But you survived, you came home safe.'

'What about your dad? And your friend's dad? Did they both make it back in one piece?'

Philip thought about the nights when his father woke the household with his screams. He's had a bad dream his mother would say and there would be no mention of it in the morning.

'Not all injuries are on the outside, are they?' Philip said. 'I don't know about Ronnie's father. Do you think that's why Ronnie doesn't want to go to war, because he's seen the damage the fighting did to his dad?'

'That's the great thing about dogs.'

Philip was confused. It seemed that Joseph was answering another question entirely.

'Take Shep here.' Joseph pointed to the dog. 'He trusts me to keep him out of danger, he's learned that I won't ask him to do something that will bring him harm; he doesn't question it. But your friend, Ronnie, well, it sounds to me like he has a questioning mind. He's trying to work out what's right – not for everyone else, but for him.'

'But he will bring shame on his family, he could even go to prison.'

The wind had changed direction, blowing the snowflakes behind them as they approached the steps. Joseph put his hand up to indicate they should wait before continuing.

'Here's another way of thinking of it,' Joseph said. 'Take us three. Together we're strong, we're helping each other reach safety.'

'You're helping me. I'm not sure I'm doing much.'

'How about if I told you that I don't see so well. I rely on Shep, he relies on me. But when the snow started to fall so heavily, well I'll admit to you, lad, I was fearful. It's easy to lose your bearings on these hills.'

'Was your sight damaged during the war?'

'All warfare is cruel, but back then it wasn't just the trenches you had to cope with. There was the poison gas.'

'And it was a gas attack that blinded you?'

'I can see shapes right enough, but when the snow falls, well everything looks the same. So you see, lad, you being here is a big help.'

'And that's what you'd say to Ronnie, if you met him? That's what I should say to him? That he needs to go to help the others he'll be fighting with?'

'Maybe. You'll know the right thing to say when you next see him.'

'What if I can't find him? What if he's injured somewhere, like I was before you and Shep came to help me?'

'Your friend believes in peace. Maybe that's what he's gone in search of.'

'But where?'

'Who would he turn to if he thought he needed to clear his conscience?'

'The priest?'

'You might have your answer right there, lad.'

6

All that Philip wanted to do when he limped through the back door of his home was to fall into the armchair in front of the fire and rest. Every muscle ached and every part of his body was chilled.

His mother didn't know which part of him to tend first; whether to strip him of his wet clothes, warm him with hot tea and crumpets, or bathe his swollen ankle with vinegar water to bring out the bruise. Part of her wanted to shout at him, beat her hands on his chest and reprimand him for taking such a risk.

And then there was Joseph. He hovered at the back door, unwilling at first to enter, until she took his arm and encouraged him in to stand in front of the coal fire. She stopped him from worrying about removing his boots and pressed a mug of hot tea into his hands, ladling sugar into it without even asking him. He had brought her boy home, sugared tea was the very least she could offer him.

Shep was content to lie at his master's feet, keeping one eye open for any biscuit crumb that may land beside him and one ear cocked ready for a command.

Jessica sat at Philip's feet, any thoughts of hair plaits a distant memory now that her brother was home. She hadn't let her mum know how scared she had been. Phil was more important to her than anything, but if she told him she guessed he would laugh at her for being silly.

'I can't sit here, mum. I still have to find Ronnie,' Philip moved his ankle a little in one direction, testing to see at what point the pain became unbearable.

'You're going nowhere.' She had her hand on her son's shoulder, pushing him back into the armchair at the same time as he tried to stand.

'I need to speak to the priest.'

'Ronnie's mother was here, with the children. But then she thought Ronnie might go home so they left just a little while ago. She doesn't know where to be, poor woman.' Helen stared into the flames of the fire. She felt as though the day would not end well. 'Why do you need to speak to the priest?'

'Philip thinks his friend may have gone to the church,' Joseph said. He was also gazing into the flames as he spoke, his head bowed a little, enjoying the warmth rising from the hot tea. He could sense the blood flowing back into his face.

'I'll go then,' Helen said. 'You're not going out again, not with that limp. You'll stay here and rest.'

She didn't wait for a reply, but moved out into the hallway, returning with her thick winter coat in one hand and gloves and scarf in the other.

'It'll be dark soon, mum. You hate being out after blackout.'

'I'll go with your mother, lad. Shep and I will keep her safe, won't we boy?'

Joseph ruffled the hair on the dog's back, which was still damp from the melted snow.

'But you can't...' Philip paused, not missing the stern glance that Joseph gave him.

'I'll be watching for your mother and she'll be watching for me. And Shep will watch for the both of us.' He put his empty mug down on the hearth and clipped Shep's lead on to his collar.

'No.' Philip's voice even startled Shep who stood beside his master, not knowing if this was a command he had to follow. 'I can't let you go without me. Ronnie is my friend and friends look out for each other. Joseph, you and I made it all the way back from Tidehaven, we can make it to St Mary's. I'll be fine, mum.'

Helen passed her scarf to her son. She understood the importance of friendship.

'I'll have hot soup for you on your return. Just come home safe.'

As the threesome left the house, negotiating the snowy pavements with care, Philip wondered if it was those words his mother used when her husband went off to fight, in the first war, and now again in this second one. Perhaps she offered a silent prayer. And now it was Philip's turn to hope that prayer had drawn his friend to the church of St Mary's in the Castle.

St Mary's stood in the heart of Tamarisk Bay, with a commanding position, overlooking the sea. Whoever designed and built it aimed to make a statement by not only building a church, but by putting it as the centrepiece of a crescent of buildings. Without the snow and without the limp it took Philip less than half an hour to reach the church from home. But now, with the fading light, and the persistent snowfall making progress at best precarious, Philip realised it would be well past blackout by the time they reached their destination.

As the sky darkened, the moon began to work its magic, creating a scene that would have made the perfect Christmas card. The streets were deserted and the snow covering meant that their progress was silenced. With no birdsong and no traffic noise, the rhythmic sound of the seawater splashing up onto the shingle formed the background music as they made their way along the last piece of seafront until they reached the ramp at the western end of the crescent, which led to the door of the church. This wasn't a time for conversation, all their concentration was focused on negotiating any obstacles along the way; obstacles for a boy with a limp and a man with failing sight.

When they reached the church doorway Joseph pushed hard on the heavy wooden door before it gave way and let them in from the outer dark to the inner gloom. Ahead of them, in the shadows, they watched Father John as he made his way up the left-hand side of the church, lighting the tall candles positioned at the end of each pew. The taper flickered as he stopped for a moment, waiting for each candle wick to catch. Then he crossed in front of the altar, bending his head momentarily in a silent prayer, before turning to make his way down the right-hand side of the church. As he turned he saw the little group standing just in front of the entrance, hesitating.

'Pip.'

It was when Philip joined Sunday school, at the age of six, that Father John decided he reminded him of his younger brother, Pip. Just recently Philip had learned that Father John's brother died in the Battle of Passchendaele, a discovery that made Philip sway between feeling proud and feeling scared.

'The lad here is looking for his friend. The church seems like a good place to come to when you have questions that no-one else can answer.' Joseph walked towards Father John and extended his hand. The priest beckoned to them both to follow him through to the sacristy. Shep led the way, his nose twitching, seeking familiar smells. Philip breathed in the sweetness of incense that permeated the priest's clothing. As older choir boys Ronnie and Philip would often lead the younger ones up the aisle, proud to be following Father John as he swung the thurible back and forth, releasing the curls of smoke that blessed the congregation.

Once they were inside the sacristy the priest gestured to them to sit. The wooden chairs were utilitarian and there were just two. Father John remained standing.

'What have you done to your leg, Pip?'

'The lad was so keen on finding his friend seems like he took one risk too many,' Joseph said. There was an impatience in his voice that Philip hadn't heard before.

'I thought he might be up at the caves. We used to go there sometimes.' Philip's explanation petered out as if he was thinking of excuses.

The priest paced a little around the edges of the sacristy, but the limitations of the room meant that once he had taken a few steps in one direction he soon had to turn back.

'Do you know where Ronnie is, Father? Have you spoken to him?'

All three were thinking of the confidentiality of the confessional, the sharing of private thoughts between parishioner and priest. But surely other conversations weren't governed in the same way?

Father John cleared his throat. Philip had heard him do it on many occasions, when he prepared himself to read the weekly sermon. It was as if the throat clearing helped him to clear his mind too.

'Ronnie will be pleased to see you.'

'He's here?' Philip jumped up, momentarily forgetting that he didn't have two strong legs to support him.

'Mind yourself there, lad.' Joseph put his arm out to steady his young friend. 'There, you see. It'll all come right in the end, you see if it doesn't.'

'Where is he, Father? Has he been here all this time?'

The priest nodded towards another door at the far end of the sacristy that Philip knew led down to the crypt. He had never investigated the underground rooms, but his imagination had created a picture of dusty tombs and skeletons.

'He's not down there, is he? He'll be scared and cold. I must go to him.'

Philip tried to shake off Joseph's grip on his arm, but as he did so he realised the priest was smiling.

'Do you think I'd leave him in the cold and dark? Pip, Ronnie is fine. You won't be able to manage the steps, so let me go down and fetch him. I have no idea how you got back from the caves and negotiated the snow blizzard, it must have been frightening for you.'

'It was only because of Joseph…'

'Seems like he's true to his namesake then. It's just around now when another Joseph was helping Our Lady to find sanctuary.'

'That Joseph had a donkey, but we have Shep.'

At the sound of his name the collie gave a loud bark, made louder still from being inside such a still, small room.

A few moments later Ronnie sat beside Philip. Joseph, Shep and Father John left the boys alone to talk.

It was a long time since Joseph had been inside a church. He hadn't forgotten the reasons he'd stopped going to mass. They were all tied up with a feeling that God had let him down. So many men died in the trenches, men he had made fought alongside, made friends with. But now, sitting in the pew beside the quiet priest, he remembered all the reasons to give thanks. He had come home. Maybe his eyes didn't work so well, but he had all his limbs. Perhaps God hadn't abandoned him after all.

Meanwhile, in the sacristy, the boys weren't thinking about God.

'Your mum's in a bad way. So is Gracie.' Philip stated the facts without judgement.

'I thought it would be easier to disappear.'

'Who for?' He held his friend's gaze, trying to read his thoughts, but failing. 'Did you think you'd hole up here forever, until the war is over?'

'I didn't think beyond this week. I suppose I thought if they couldn't find me, then they would forget about me. There's plenty ready to fight, Philip, you know that. One less won't make any difference.'

'You know it doesn't work like that. If they let one person say no, then it opens up that route for others. We all have to stand together, that's the only way we can show Hitler we mean business.'

If he could have stood to reinforce the message he would have done so. Instead he waved his arms around as if he was directing his very own troop of soldiers.

'Killing young German men, who are just like you and me, doesn't mean we'll defeat Hitler. It's not the right way to do it, Phil. There has to be another way.'

'Nobody wants to fight, but sometimes there's no choice.'

'We've all got choices. You wait until it's your turn. If the war isn't over by the time you turn eighteen, what then?'

Philip hadn't thought about it. The war would be over soon, wouldn't it? And yet the last war had gone for more than four years. The troops died in their millions and now it was all happening again. Nothing had changed. Maybe Ronnie was right.

'What does Father John say?'

'He just listens. He says it's not his place to advise. But the church doesn't hold with killing, does it? It's the sixth Commandment.'

'Maybe there's an exception to the rule when you're dealing with a mad man? What are you going to do,

Ronnie? I can't lie to your mum. I'll have to tell her where you are.'

Ronnie shrugged his shoulders.

'Shall I bring your mum here? Has Father John said you can stay with him?'

'I'm not being fair, am I? I wanted to save my family from recriminations and accusations. People around here won't look kindly on a conscientious objector. I don't care for myself, but it's not right they should be punished.'

'If word gets out you're here then you'll get Father John into trouble for hiding you. It's time for you to make a decision, Ron. Whatever you do, I'll back you all the way.'

In the Chandler household Helen was feeling she had let her family down. Tomorrow it would be Christmas Eve and every year on that day she would spend the hours leading up to midnight making the mince pies and preparing the vegetables and stuffing for Christmas dinner. Philip and Jessica would sit at the kitchen table and try to sneak a piece or two of raw carrot when Helen wasn't looking. It was the bliss of normality.

But these last few days Helen had been so worried about Ronnie going missing and about Philip's escapades to St Clement's Caves that she'd forgotten to buy half the things she always bought in the last few days before Christmas.

Besides the worries over the boys, it didn't seem right to be doing normal things when British ships had been sunk by U-boats in the Scapa Flow. Families had lost loved ones and who knew what horrors were yet to come.

She'd lost her temper with Jessica and then regretted it. Her daughter had been on and on about the Christmas tree when decorations were the very last thing on her mind. But Jess was still just a young girl. Every year she looked forward to the moment she was allowed to place the angel on the top spike of the Christmas tree. Then the family would take it in turns to add the baubles and tinsel, until every branch was festooned with colour. This year George wasn't there to fetch a tree and now that Philip had wrecked his ankle he wouldn't be able to carry a tree either.

These thoughts of trees and mince pies were interrupted when the back door swung open and Philip hobbled in, followed by Ronnie and Joseph, with Shep bringing up the rear.

'Oh, you're safe,' was all she could think of to say as she extended her arms out to the two boys, not knowing who she was more pleased to see. 'But Ronnie, you shouldn't be here, you need to go straight home. Your mother is making herself ill with worrying about you.'

'I had to make sure Philip got back okay. It's my fault he's hurt his ankle.'

'I told the lad I would have seen him home safe, but Ronnie would have none of it,' Joseph said, stomping his boots on the doormat. The snow had crept under the back door and laid in a line along the full width of the doorway, decorating it just like cake icing. Shep looked more like a husky than a black and white sheepdog and as he made his way towards the stove he shook with such energy that he sent a shower of snow crystals around the kitchen.

'Will we see you at church tomorrow night, Ronnie?' Helen called out as Ronnie headed back out into the snow. She didn't expect a reply. Once the boy had been welcomed back into his family home there would be difficult conversations and impossible decisions to make.

7

Clara barely had time to hug her son close to her before Gracie squeezed herself between the two of them, wanting to know where her big brother had been.

'I've been waiting to send my letter to Santa and tomorrow is Christmas Eve. He'll need time to read it and get my presents ready.'

'Away with you now, Gracie. Ronnie's cold and tired, we need to make him something warm to drink before we can worry about your Christmas presents.'

Once Ronnie was settled in front of the fire, Gracie plumped herself down on his lap. 'We put the letter on the fire, don't we, Ronnie? You did it for me last year, do you remember?'

Ronnie had spoken very little since being welcomed back into his home and family. His thoughts revolved around overwhelming feelings of guilt. His mother's face was pale and drawn. He doubted she had slept since he'd run away. His best friend had wrecked his ankle and now his precious Gracie, his darling little sister, was worrying about her letter to Santa.

But it was another letter that sat unopened on the mantelpiece that had started all of this.

'Gracie, where are Bobby and Jemima? Why don't you go and play with them for a while. Leave Ronnie to have his tea in peace.'

Reluctantly Gracie climbed off her brother's lap and went in search of her new friends, who had stayed out of the way in the sitting room. It seemed this family had enough problems to deal with without their presence complicating matters further.

Clara poured her son a strong cup of tea, stirred a spoonful of sugar into it and then set about making a jam sandwich. Ronnie's favourite. She moved around the kitchen, preparing a tray, setting the cup and saucer beside the tea plate, keeping an ear alert for any sound coming from the sitting room.

She carried the tray through, but before she could put it down on the footstool, Ronnie stood and took it from her. He put it onto the sideboard, then pulled his mother towards him, wrapping his arms around her waist.

'I'm so sorry, mum. I've made a real mess of everything.'

Clara could feel tears pricking at the edges of her eyes. She didn't have the right words for her son, she guessed at his questions but knew she would have no answers.

'Have your sandwich now and drink your tea while it's hot.' She pushed him away gently and moved to the far side of the fireplace. The envelope on the mantelpiece seemed to be taunting them both.

'You know why I went, don't you, mum?'

'I think I understand, yes. But I don't know what to tell you, Ronnie. It's the law. You can't go breaking the law. There will be terrible consequences.'

Clara had heard what happened to conscientious objectors, but only on the radio news bulletins. There was no-one in Tamarisk Bay who had refused to fight. Or at least no-one she knew. Until now.

'I'm not worried for me, mum. It's you and Gracie I worry about.'

'If you go off to fight?'

'No, if I don't.'

'Think about it for a few more days. Tomorrow is Christmas Eve. No-one will expect you to leave your family over Christmas. At least wait until after Boxing Day. They can't begrudge you that.'

By the time the tea was drunk and there were not even crumbs remaining of the sandwich Clara had made a decision. Holding onto Ronnie's hand she led him into the hallway, taking his coat from the understairs cupboard and passing it to him. She put her own coat on, then her gloves and scarf.

'Where are we going, mum?'

She didn't reply, but pulled him close beside her as they walked along Victoria Road and down First Avenue, then into Second Avenue and up the footpath towards the house where Mr Yardley lived. Ernest Yardley taught the children of Tamarisk Bay until they told him he couldn't teach any more. But even in retirement he continued to help out by giving private lessons to those who struggled with their reading and writing. Ronnie had always been a little in awe of him, perhaps because he was a giant of a man at six feet, six inches, with a mass of black hair and a bushy beard. His booming voice commanded attention so he never had need to resort to the punishments that some of the other teachers threatened the children with.

Ronnie had never been inside Mr Yardley's house and had never met his wife, a diminutive mouse-like woman, with a high-pitched voice and gaps in her teeth when she smiled. She welcomed the visitors into the sitting room, the blast of heat from the inglenook fireplace driving them to peel off their layers before they sat on the comfiest settee that Ronnie had ever sat on.

'We are so sorry to disturb you,' Clara began, but Mabel Yardley waved her hand to dismiss the apology and disappeared into the kitchen, calling out to her husband, 'Visitors, Ernie.'

When Ernest joined them in the sitting room, Ronnie was surprised to see the bushy beard had gone; instead a neatly combed moustache made the man look younger and more affable.

Over the next hour, several cups of tea were drunk and, despite Clara's protestations, two mince pies each were enjoyed. Clara was right when she guessed that Ernest Yardley would know about the law, he would know what Ronnie's options were, if indeed there were any options.

It seemed that Ronnie would have to justify his position to a tribunal, who would allocate him to one of three categories: unconditional exemption; exemption conditional upon performing specified civilian work, which might be farming or helping out in the local hospital; or exemption from fighting only. This would mean Ronnie could join a non-combatant corps like the Royal Army Medical Corp. Ernest explained the possibilities and watched as Helen clung to her son's hand, thankful that the boy might escape prison. Ronnie absorbed the words. He didn't have to abandon his beliefs, he could still help his friends, his country, but wouldn't be asked to kill.

It seemed that this Christmas might be a time for celebration after all.

Just a little after 11pm on Christmas Eve the Chandler family held hands as they made their way along the dark snowy streets towards St Mary's in the Castle. Philip walked on one side of his mother, Jessica on the other. In his right hand Philip lent on the walking stick that Joseph had left with him, despite the boy's protestations. Philip didn't like to think about what it would be like to have failing sight. Even in the dark he liked being able to make out familiar shapes of houses, trees, all the landmarks of his home town that formed the map of his life so far.

'Will you come to midnight mass, Joseph?' Philip had asked the old man before he left.

The old man hadn't answered, but Philip hoped he would be there, just as he hoped that Ronnie would be there in his regular place, beside his mother and Gracie, in the fourth pew back from the altar on the right-hand side of the church. Only then could he be certain that all would be well, even though he knew in his heart that nothing could be the same for any of them. It wasn't just the war that was changing things.

'Slow up, Jessica. Your brother can't rush, we need to go at his pace.' Helen could sense her daughter's excitement, she could barely keep her hand still as her mother held onto it.

'But it's nearly Christmas.' Now that Ronnie had been found and Philip's ankle was on the mend, all Jessica could think about was whether Santa would bring the ribbons she longed for, ribbons that she would plait through her hair. She'd been practising for days, using ribbons she'd borrowed from her friend, Lucy. Of course, she knew Santa wasn't real, she'd known that for ages, ever since she woke early one Christmas morning to see her dad laying parcels at the foot of her bed. Thinking about her dad made her feel so sad that she almost forgot about the ribbons.

Philip was thinking of his father too. Earlier that evening his mother had made the mince pies as usual; his father's favourite. She had knocked on their neighbour's back door and asked if they had any spare mincemeat. There was just enough for four mince pies. One for each of them and one for Joseph. They had persuaded him to join them for

Christmas dinner with the promise of a sausage or two for Shep. Philip said a silent prayer that his father would have a moment to enjoy Christmas, in between the guns and the terror.

They reached the front door of the church and joined another group of parishioners who had made their way up the eastern side of the slope. There was a hubbub of anticipation as someone ahead of them pushed open the door to see the church bathed in candlelight. The cold draught that came in alongside the people caused the candles to flicker, creating shadows that moved as though they were alive.

The Chandler family made their way to their regular pew, Philip went in first by sitting and sliding along, before turning to look for his friend. The pew behind them was empty. But at the back of the church he spotted Joseph and Shep arriving. He waved to them, not knowing what to feel; pleased that his new friend was there, disappointed that Ronnie was not.

Then Father John appeared beside Philip, touching his arm, before bending down to talk quietly to him.

'What did he say?' Helen asked, once the priest had moved away.

'Ronnie is here. He and his mum have been talking to the priest.' Philip could guess at the conversation, gratitude that the priest had kept Ronnie safe, but maybe also asking for guidance. But it wasn't Father John's place to offer guidance this time, this wasn't a matter of faith, of belief. Or perhaps it was.

Then the Barnard family emerged from the sacristy. Ronnie led the way, followed by his mother and sister and the two newest members of the family, Bobby and Jemima. All had their heads bowed, except Gracie who was looking all around as if she hoped that Santa would appear right there in front of the altar.

As they slid into their pew Philip turned, holding his hand out to Ronnie, but no words were exchanged. This wasn't a time for questions, the mass was about to start.

Every pew was full, with a few people standing at the back of the church. The congregation sang heartily, pleased for the temporary cheer that familiar tunes brought them. *'God rest ye merry gentlemen'* was the first carol to be sung. The candlelight didn't offer enough light for people to read the words, but no-one needed the hymn books, they knew the verses as well as they knew their favourite nursery rhymes.

The mass continued, with prayers, more singing and then it was time for Father John's Christmas sermon. He had thought long and hard about what to say to his congregation. This was a troubled time for everyone. Many had seen loved ones go off to fight and couldn't be certain if they would see them again. And here, in the heart of his community, was a young boy who was struggling. Which words would help all of them cope with the weeks, months, maybe even years to come?

He cleared his throat. There was silence in the church, except for Gracie, who chose this moment to make a loud sneeze, which made everyone smile.

Then Father John spoke:

'Christmas is a time for family' he said. 'Now more than ever we need each other. This congregation is a family, as is this town. We can even think of our country as being one big family, all looking out for each other. Together we are so much stronger, as a community, as a country. And just like before there will be others in distant countries who will support us, be our Allies. And that is why we will succeed, because when we are divided we are weak, but when we stand together we are strong.'

The congregation stood as one, reflecting Father John's words.

Clara stood beside her son in the church, as they sang the last carol of the service, taking his hand and squeezing it tight. And as the congregation bellowed out each verse of *'It came upon the midnight clear'*, there was just one line that Ronnie and Philip sang louder than all the rest: *'Peace on the earth, goodwill to men'.*

By the same author

Readers who are familiar with the *Sussex Crime* novels will know that Philip Chandler is Janie Juke's father. Here, in *Divided we Fall* we meet Philip when he is just a lad, right at the start of the Second World War.

If you are new to Isabella Muir's *Sussex Crime* series and you would like to read more then look out for the full-length novels in the series:

BOOK 1: THE TAPESTRY BAG
BOOK 2: LOST PROPERTY
BOOK 3: THE INVISIBLE CASE

Praise for the *Sussex Crime* series

'This was a great find. A librarian turns to sleuthing in 1960s England. Janie Juke, an Agatha Christie enthusiast, is a very likeable protagonist. A real page turner. I've already bought the next book in the series… hoping there will be many more to come.'

'I got straight into the story … I really like the way the author depicted the 60s …I felt as if I was there!'

'Intriguing detective story with lovely period setting and interesting characters. I'm looking forward to seeing what Janie Juke solves next.'

'Loved every page and didn't want to put it down. Can't wait until the next one in the series.'

'Thoroughly enjoyable book. Kept me interested till the end. Looking forward to the next one.'

'The glimpses into WW2 are particularly good. Solid writing, great story, and Janie as a character is growing on me. I hope there are more in the series.'

About the author

Isabella rediscovered her love of writing fiction during two happy years working on and completing her MA in Professional Writing.

The setting for the Sussex Crime mystery series is based on the area where Isabella was born and lived most of her life. When she thinks of Tamarisk Bay she pictures her birthplace in St Leonards-on-Sea, East Sussex and its surroundings.

Aside from her love of words, Isabella has a love of all things caravan-like. She has enjoyed several years travelling in the UK and abroad. Now, Isabella and her husband run a small campsite in West Sussex.

Her faithful companion, Scottish terrier Hamish, is never far from her side.

Find out more about Isabella, her published books, as well as her forthcoming titles at: **www.isabellamuir.com** and follow Isabella on Twitter: **@SussexMysteries**

By the same author

THE TAPESTRY BAG
LOST PROPERTY
THE INVISIBLE CASE
THE FORGOTTEN CHILDREN
IVORY VELLUM: A COLLECTION OF SHORT STORIES

Lightning Source UK Ltd.
Milton Keynes UK
UKHW011959300619
345322UK00001B/5/P

9 781872 889184